by Fran Manushkin

illustrated by Laura Zarrin

Raintree is an imprint of Capstone Global Library Limited, a company incorporated in England and Wales having its registered office at 264 Banbury Road, Oxford, OX2 7DY – Registered company number: 6695582

www.raintree.co.uk
myorders@raintree.co.uk

Text © Capstone Global Library Limited 2021
The moral rights of the proprietor have been asserted.

Original illustrations © Capstone Global Library Limited 2021
Originated by Capstone Global Library Ltd
Printed and bound in India

978 1 4747 9450 3

British Library Cataloguing in Publication Data
A full catalogue record for this book is available from the British Library.

Contents

Katie's Neighbourhood

Police

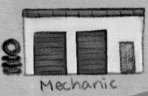

Library

Mechanic

City
Hall

Grocery Store

Post Office

Chapter 1
Is it fun to be a farmer?

In the summer, Katie and
her friends loved going to
the farmers' market.

Every Sunday they found
new foods to taste.

"Come and meet my aunt Carmen," said Pedro. "She's a new farmer at the market."

"Hi!" said Katie. "Is it fun to be a farmer?"

"You can find out," said

Aunt Carmen. "Come and

stay overnight next Saturday.

You can help bring my

vegetables to the market."

"That's cool!" said Katie.

"I love tomatoes. Maybe I
can help to pick them."

"Certainly," said Farmer
Carmen.

Chapter 2
The tasty farm

On Saturday morning, Pedro's dad drove Katie, JoJo and Pedro to Aunt Carmen's farm. It was a long way.

"Welcome!" called Farmer Carmen. "Let me show you around."

Katie saw long, long rows of lettuce and purple and green cabbages.

"Uh-oh," said Katie.

"I can't see any tomatoes."

"Don't worry," said

Farmer Carmen. "They are

over here. Pick a big one

and take a bite."

"Wow!" Katie shouted.

"It's juicy, juicy, JUICY!"

Aunt Carmen smiled.

"My tomatoes have passed

the test. They are perfect for

market tomorrow."

Pedro joked, "These cucumbers have got goosebumps. They must be cold."

Katie joked back, "They are excited about going to the market."

Katie and JoJo helped

Farmer Carmen pick tomatoes.

Pedro liked picking peppers.

He also liked saying, "Pedro is

picking peppers" over and over.

Dinner was a tasty salad.

"Let's go to bed early,"

said Farmer Carmen. "We

must wake up at four o'clock

to pack up my veggies to

take to the market."

Chapter 3

Farmers' market day

It was still dark when

Katie woke up. She saw

Farmer Carmen and her

helpers packing vegetables

into baskets. They loaded

the baskets onto the truck.

Katie saw the sunrise

as they drove to the market.

She yawned and yawned.

"I don't think farmers sleep

very much," she said.

At the market, JoJo and Pedro stacked up cabbages. Katie tucked tomatoes into pretty baskets.

Pedro said, "Aunt Carmen

works so hard. I hope we sell

everything."

"We will," said Katie.

But she was a bit worried.

There was so much to sell!

Miss Winkle wanted lots
of tomatoes.

Katie told her, "I picked
some and packed them."

"Well done!" said Miss
Winkle.

Katie sold carrots to Sharon, the postwoman. Mr Nelson got lettuce and cabbage for his grocery shop.

But at closing time, a lot

of the vegetables hadn't sold.

"This is sad," said Pedro.

"Very sad!" said JoJo.

"Wait!" yelled Katie. "Look

who's coming!"

It was Haley O'Hara and
her five brothers and sisters.

"Yay!" yelled Haley. "We're
not too late for veggies."

They filled seven bags.

No vegetables were left!

Katie told Farmer Carmen,

"You work very hard!"

"But my work is tasty,"

said Farmer Carmen. They

shared the very last tomato.

It was very tasty!

Glossary

cabbage a large vegetable with green or purple leaves shaped into a round head

cucumber a long, green salad vegetable with a soft centre filled with seeds

farmers' market a shopping area where people sell the items they grow

lettuce a green, leafy salad vegetable

tomato a red, juicy fruit eaten as a vegetable either raw or cooked

Katie's questions

1. What traits make a good farmer? Would you like to be a farmer? Why or why not?

2. In the first chapter, Katie asks Farmer Carmen if it is fun to be a farmer. Does Farmer Carmen think farming is fun? What about Katie? Do you think it would be fun to be a farmer?

3. List as many vegetables as you can. How many did you list? Which one is your favourite?

4. Imagine you have your own stall at a farmers' market. What would you sell? Draw a picture of your farmers' market stand.

Katie interviews Farmer Carmen

Katie: Hi Farmer Carmen! Thanks for talking to me about being a farmer. I'm curious . . . what do you like best about being a farmer?

Farmer Carmen: As you know, Katie, there are so many great things about being a farmer. I love working outside in the fresh air and sunshine. And I love working with my hands. But the thing I love best is growing food that feeds people in my community and beyond.

Katie: How do farmers decide what to grow?

Farmer Carmen: The plants we grow need to be right for the climate. That means how hot it usually is and how much rain we get. Some plants need lots of sunshine. Others grow better in cooler places. But not all farmers grow things.

Katie: If they're not growing things, what do they do?

Farmer Carmen: They raise things! The animals that farmers raise are called livestock. Some livestock is raised for meat, and some is raised for the things they give us.

Katie: What do you mean "give us"?

Farmer Carmen: Like chickens give us eggs, and sheep give us wool.

Katie: And cows give us milk!

Farmer Carmen: That's right, Katie. You learn so quickly. You'd make a great farmer.

Katie: Thanks! So, what would I need to do if I decided that I wanted to be a farmer for real?

Farmer Carmen: Most farmers are trained by working on farms. There's no better way to learn, if you ask me. Some people study farming at college too.

Katie: Well, thanks again for talking to me. And big thanks for working so hard to feed all of us! You are the best!

Farmer Carmen: Thanks, Katie. I think you are pretty great too!

About the author

Fran Manushkin is the author of many popular picture books. There is a real Katie Woo - she's Fran's great-niece - but she never gets in half the trouble of the Katie Woo in the books. Fran writes in New York City, USA, without the help of her two naughty cats, Chaim and Goldy.

About the illustrator

Laura Zarrin spent her early childhood in the St. Louis, Missouri, area in the USA. There she explored creeks, woods and attic closets, climbed trees, and dug for artifacts in the garden, all in preparation for her future career as an archaeologist. She never became one, however, because she realised she's much happier drawing in the comfort of her own home while watching TV. When she was 12, her family moved to the Silicon Valley in California, where she still resides with her very logical husband and teen sons, and their illogical dog, Cody.